I'm a SUPERVEGAN

A confidence-building children's book for our littlest vegans

Written by **Katie Clark**
Illustrated by **Sonnaz**

Wouldn't it be super if everyone were vegan?
Living in a world we could truly believe in?
A big change starts small, with everyday choices.
Let's work together, be heroes for the voiceless.

Longview Ink

Copyright © 2019 by Katie Clark   All rights reserved   Published by Longview Ink   www.LongviewInk.com
Special discounts are available on quantity purchases by corporations, associations, and others. For details, contact the publisher through the website above

Names: Clark, Katie, author. | Sonnaz, illustrator.
Title: I'm a supervegan : a confidence-building children's book for our littlest vegans /
text and art direction by Katie Clark ; illustrations by Sonnaz.
Description: Reynoldsburg, OH : Longview Ink, 2019. | Summary: Through vibrant illustrations and
playful rhymes, this book uses the wonder of childhood imagination to show Elizabeth's journey through self-doubt to supervegan.
Identifiers: LCCN 2019902105 | ISBN 978-1-7337553-0-6 (paperback) | ISBN 978-0-578-45226-5
(hardcover) | ISBN 978-1-7337553-1-3 (ebook)
Subjects: LCSH: Picture books for children. | Veganism--Juvenile fiction. | CYAC: Stories in rhyme. |
Self-confidence--Fiction. | Nutrition--Fiction. | BISAC: JUVENILE FICTION / Health & Daily Living /
General. | JUVENILE FICTION / Cooking & Food. | JUVENILE FICTION / Social Themes / Self-
Esteem & Self-Reliance. | JUVENILE FICTION / Stories in Verse.
Classification: LCC PZ7.1.C563 Im 2019 (print) | LCC PZ7.1.C563 (ebook) | DDC [Fic]--dc23

Text and Art Direction by Katie Clark   Illustrations by Sonnaz   Design by Juan Lara

Mom, can I be a superhero when I grow up?
Elizabeth, you already are, sweetheart!
You're a supervegan-

brave, caring, and smart.

But Mom–
am I really brave?

Yes!
Some people eat animals,
but you're proud to eat plants.

The animals are cheering –
look up in the stands!

You ask,
"Is this vegan?"
when offered a snack.

If the answer is no, you smile, say
"No thank you,"
and hand it back.

You always try foods with names that sound odd -

dragon fruit,

horned melon,

wild rice-

bring it on!

But Mom –
am I *really* caring?

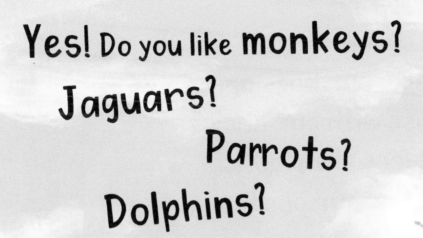

Yes! Do you like **monkeys?**
Jaguars?
Parrots?
Dolphins?

Vegans protect the rainforests they belong in.

Reusing our bags and
being wise with our choices
reduces the plastic
polluting our oceans.

Cows have hearts that
feel sadness, just
like me and you.

You don't drink cow's milk, because calves need their mommies too.

But Mom –
am I *really* smart?

Yes!
You've learned we don't need
animals to make our favorite treats. We bake
them at home using fruits, nuts, beans, and seeds.

Animals are not good for
our bodies, as you know.

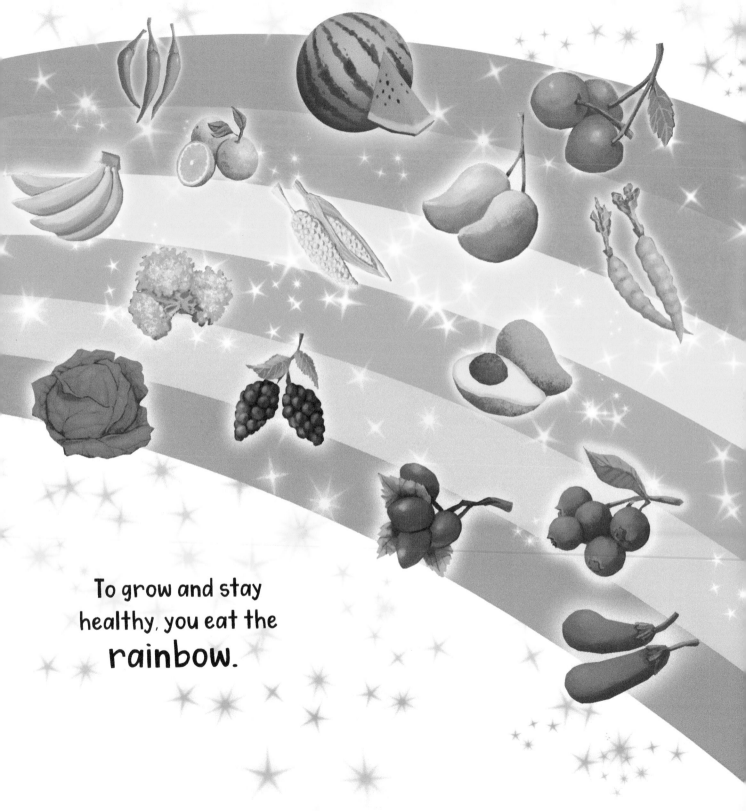

To grow and stay
healthy, you eat the
rainbow.

You grow berries **SO** high **SO** huge you can barely reach.

But afterwards,
a sweet reward-
time to stuff
your cheeks!

Wow-
I *am* a supervegan!
I save animals every day!

Do you want to be a supervegan?
Yes? That's great!

Katie Clark

Katie Clark is wife to Caleb and mom to supervegans Elizabeth and Clara. Katie set out to write vegan books for children when she wanted a creative way to assure her own daughters that being vegan is brave, caring, and smart. Katie hopes every child who reads her books will feel confident and empowered through their choice to be vegan.

Katie has a Masters in Business Administration, which came in handy during her previous analytics career. Nowadays, she teaches piano and ESL on top of being a stay at home mom, author, and homeschool teacher. Katie loves to spend time with her daughters going on nature walks, visiting museums, and hanging out at the library. Katie is also passionate about helping others incorporate more plant-based meals into their diets.

You can follow Katie on social media @weRsupervegans.

For more information about her books, visit her website at www.wearesupervegans.com.

OUR FAVORITE BANANA BREAD RECIPE—ENJOY!

One Bowl Strawberry Banana Bread

- 4 medium ripe bananas
- 1/2 cup (120ml) almond milk (or other non-dairy milk)
- 3 Tbsp (45g) unsweetened applesauce (or 1/4 cup/60ml oil)
- 1 tsp vanilla extract
- 2 cups (250g) all-purpose or whole wheat flour
- 1/2 cup (100g) brown sugar
- 1/4 cup granulated sugar
- 3 tsp baking powder
- 1/4 tsp salt
- 1 tsp ground cinnamon
- 1/2 cup (160g) strawberry jam

Preheat oven to 350°F (180°C). Mash bananas in a large bowl. Stir in almond milk, applesauce, and vanilla extract. Stir in dry ingredients until mixed well. Pour 2/3 of the batter into a greased loaf pan. Spread jam over mixture. Pour in the rest and bake for 60 minutes.

Lightning Source UK Ltd.
Milton Keynes UK
UKHW020956101221
395384UK00002B/50